# My Dog Zeke

**Macmillan McGraw-Hill**

New York      Farmington

The thing I wanted most in the world was a dog of my own. I wanted one more than anyone had ever wanted anything. Maybe it was because I had no brothers or sisters. It wasn't so much that I was lonely. I had plenty of friends to play with. But if I had a dog, it would be waiting for me whenever I came home. I could play with it on rainy days when I couldn't go out. It would stay in the house with me at night and sleep in my room, on my bed, or even under the covers with me. I didn't care what kind of dog I had. I just wanted a dog for my very own friend.

My parents didn't think that my having a dog was a good idea at all. Even though I promised to take care of it all by myself, I don't think they quite believed me.

"A dog is too much trouble," they said, "too much trouble." I tried to tell them that something you loved and were loved by couldn't possibly be too much trouble, but they still said no.

There were lots of dogs in my neighborhood. Some of them were my friends. My very favorite was a German shepherd named Rex, who belonged to Mr. Kendall. I saw them almost every day on my way home from school. Mr. Kendall lived about three miles away from my house in an old shack in the woods. Every day he and Rex walked to the little park at the end of my street and sat on the same bench.

Besides my grandparents, Mr. Kendall was the oldest person I knew. I was fascinated by his long, rough face, his old, gnarled hands, and his impossibly thin ankles. He always wore an old, tweed overcoat, even on those first warm, spring days when I couldn't wait to take my jacket off.

Rex was usually stretched out at his feet, mostly hidden under the bench except for his long nose which sometimes sniffed at passersby. When Rex saw me, he'd come out to wag his tail and say hello. Then I was glad that Mr. Kendall wore that old overcoat because its enormous pockets were stuffed with dog biscuits. He'd always slip some to me so I could give them to Rex.

In return for the biscuits, Rex would do tricks that Mr. Kendall had taught him—sit, bark, give-me-your-paw. The one I liked best was roll over, because then I could pet Rex's soft, white stomach. When I did, he'd roll his head from side to side and sometimes lick my hand. And if I stopped before Rex was ready for me to stop, he'd use his long snout to nudge my hand back to his stomach.

"You should have a dog of your own," Mr. Kendall said to me one day.

"I think so, too," I sighed, "but my parents won't let me. They say it's too much trouble."

"Well, I guess parents know best."

"Do you think so?"

Instead of answering, Mr. Kendall dug down deep into one of his pockets. "Here," he said, handing me a biscuit, "why don't you see if you can get Rex to give you his paw?"

Just when I thought I was never going to have a dog of my own, the unexpected happened—the way it sometimes does. A few weeks before Christmas, just after dinner, our doorbell rang. Suddenly there was a lot of noise coming from the living room. When I went to investigate, I found my aunt and uncle standing in the middle of the room. My aunt was holding a long leather leash. At the other end of it, was a fluffy white dog.

"His name is Zeke, and he's for you," my uncle said when he saw me staring at the dog. "Merry early Christmas!"

For a minute I was so surprised I couldn't say a word. "Really for me?" I finally asked. When my aunt and uncle both nodded yes, I was so happy I nearly cried.

My aunt let go of the leash and Zeke, who was pretty excited himself, rushed around the room, sniffing chair legs and people's legs, nosing into corners and behind curtains. I couldn't take my eyes off him. He was about two years old, not too small and not too big, with pointed ears and a pointed nose. He had a full,

white coat that ended in a beautiful banner of a tail which curled up tightly over his back. I thought he was beautiful. But he was more than beautiful. He was also remarkable because when I got close enough to hold him and look at him carefully, I saw that he had one brown eye and one blue eye! I'd never seen a dog with two different colored eyes. It was wonderful. Not only did I now have a dog of my own, but he was a very special, exceptional dog!

I could see from the way my parents looked at my aunt and uncle that they hadn't known I was going to get Zeke. And I could see they weren't impressed with his extraordinary eyes, or much else about him either. But he was a gift to me, so they didn't say anything. I kissed and hugged and thanked my aunt and uncle so much when they left our house, that they laughingly said they were "escaping."

After they'd gone, I put my arms around Zeke. "Oh, he's wonderful," I said to my parents. "I'm going to take such good care of him. You'll see," I promised when I saw the looks they exchanged. "You'll hardly know he's here."

That night, when Zeke and I were going to sleep in my room, I told him, "You'll have to be good, Zeke— very, very good so they'll let me keep you." I looked down at his soft, furry face and into his one brown eye and one blue eye, and I smiled. There wasn't a doubt in the world that Zeke was the best dog ever.

And there wasn't a doubt that I was the happiest girl in the world. As I tried to fall asleep, I said, "My dog Zeke," over and over again. I couldn't wait for morning to come so that I could take him for a walk. "This is my dog Zeke," I would say to anyone I happened to meet. As I fell asleep, it didn't seem impossible to me that Zeke was so exceptional that he would shake hands with the people and politely bark out, "Pleased to meet you." My dog Zeke.

The next morning Zeke woke me up very early by scratching at the bedroom door. I was dressed in a flash, and we went outside for a walk. No one else was up, so it was a good time to show Zeke his new neighborhood. I pointed out the spots other dogs liked best. I wasn't surprised to see that Zeke liked them too. It was our first walk together.

When we got home, my mother and father were already having breakfast. "He loves the neighborhood," I told them, taking a seat at the table. Zeke gave them each a sniff, then settled down beside my chair.

I had a few bites. Then I jumped up. "I'm too excited to eat!" I shouted. Before my parents could say a word, Zeke and I were outside again in the cold, December sunshine.

The first person I took Zeke to meet was my friend Iris, who lived next door. "Look," I cried when she opened her door, "my aunt and uncle gave me a dog for Christmas. His name is Zeke. Isn't he beautiful?"

Iris looked at him and patted his head. "Yes, he's very nice," she said. Then she stood back and pointed to the sweater she was wearing. "It's new," she told me. "How do you like it?"

"It's very pretty," I said, moving closer to Zeke. I sighed to myself. Iris wasn't going to make a fuss over my new dog. I guess she was as happy about her new sweater as I was about Zeke. That's the way it is some-times—even with friends.

"Well, we're on our way to the playground," I said. "See you later."

I decided not to take Zeke to meet my other friends. I knew he'd meet them in the next few days anyway. Zeke was *my* dog and he made *me* happy. Showing him off wasn't the important thing. Besides, I knew that nobody could be as happy as I.

On the way to the playground, I saw Mr. Kendall and Rex on their bench. Zeke saw them, too; at least he saw Rex. He pulled so hard on his leash that I had to run to keep up with him.

"What have you got there?" Mr. Kendall laughed, as I tried to untwist myself from the leash which Zeke had wound around me. Breathlessly, I told Mr. Kendall all about my new dog, and without even knowing I was going to do it, I kissed him on the cheek. "I'm so happy!" I said, sitting down next to him.

For a while, we watched Zeke and Rex getting to know each other. Then I suddenly had an idea. "Mr. Kendall," I began, choosing my words carefully, "my mother and father haven't said anything but I can tell they're not very happy about my getting Zeke. I promised I'd take care of him all by myself . . . ."

"Well, he's yours," Mr. Kendall said. "It's only right that you take care of him."

"Oh, I will, I will! But I was just thinking . . . if Zeke were as well-behaved as Rex, my parents couldn't possibly mind having him in the house. So I was wondering . . . do you think you might have the time to help me teach him things? I mean, well, you know, just how to be good?"

Mr. Kendall smiled. "Well now, I reckon I could find the time. Sure I could."

"Oh boy!" I shouted, almost kissing him again. In fact, I could have kissed the world, gobbled up the sun and the sky. "Can we start right now?"

It turned out we could. "It looks like the first thing he should learn is how to walk right next to you," Mr. Kendall decided. "That's called heeling."

"Why is it called that?"

"I guess because the dog walks right at your heels. But, you know, it could be called anything because all that matters—at least to the dog—is that you always use the same word."

"You mean I could say, umm, *orange*, and he would heel?" I thought that was very funny.

"Sure. That's the interesting thing about words. If you decide that a word means something and the person, or dog, you're talking to understands that's what you mean, you both know what you're talking about. Why, then you have your own special language."

I loved the idea. "A whole private language just for Zeke and me! That's really special!" I stood up and pulled Zeke from the bench. *"Orange, Zeke, orange,"* I commanded in a firm voice. Zeke ignored me and tried to pull me back to Rex. I pulled harder at the leash and gathered it up until I was holding him by the collar. He still wouldn't *orange.* Mr. Kendall didn't say anything. I felt awful that Zeke wouldn't do what I wanted him to and that I couldn't make him do it. What would Mr. Kendall think? I tried again. *"Orange, Zeke,"* I said in an even firmer voice, and this time, when he wouldn't stay at my side, I gave him a not-so-gentle tap on the nose. Surprised, Zeke looked up at me. "I didn't mean to do that," I said to Mr. Kendall unhappily.

He stood up and took Zeke's leash from me. "I think we'd better try a different method." He patted Zeke and talked softly to him. "You see, you have to get his attention," he said to me. "That's the first thing when you teach anybody anything." He got up and pulled the leash just enough so that Zeke was standing at his side. "Now, *orange*, Zeke, *orange*," he said and took a few steps.

At first Zeke didn't understand what Mr. Kendall wanted him to do. He pulled at the leash and tried to sniff the ground. But Mr. Kendall kept at it, and finally Zeke circled the bench at his side. After they did it one more time, Mr. Kendall gave him a small piece of biscuit and a big, hearty pat. "Good, Zeke, good," he said.

"You've got a smart dog here," Mr. Kendall told me, making me smile with pride. "He'll learn anything you want to teach him, but you've got to do it right. You see, animals are like people. If they like you, they want to please you. But you've got to be straight with them. Make sure they understand what you want them to do. If they don't get the idea right away, you've got to be patient until they do. And then you have to show them that they made you happy. That way they'll feel happy, too. You understand?" I nodded. "Now you try it."

I did just what I had seen Mr. Kendall do, but Zeke wouldn't *orange*. "Just relax," Mr. Kendall said. "We have all the time in the world."

I took a deep breath and began again. I patted Zeke and talked to him gently, and after a little while I got him to walk at my side.

When we had gone around the bench twice, I flopped down beside Zeke and threw my arms around him. "Good, Zeke, good," I laughed. He was so happy, he gave my face a hundred licks. I got up and we walked around the bench again. Zeke *oranged*. "He really understands now, doesn't he?" I asked Mr. Kendall. "It sure looks like it," he said with a smile.

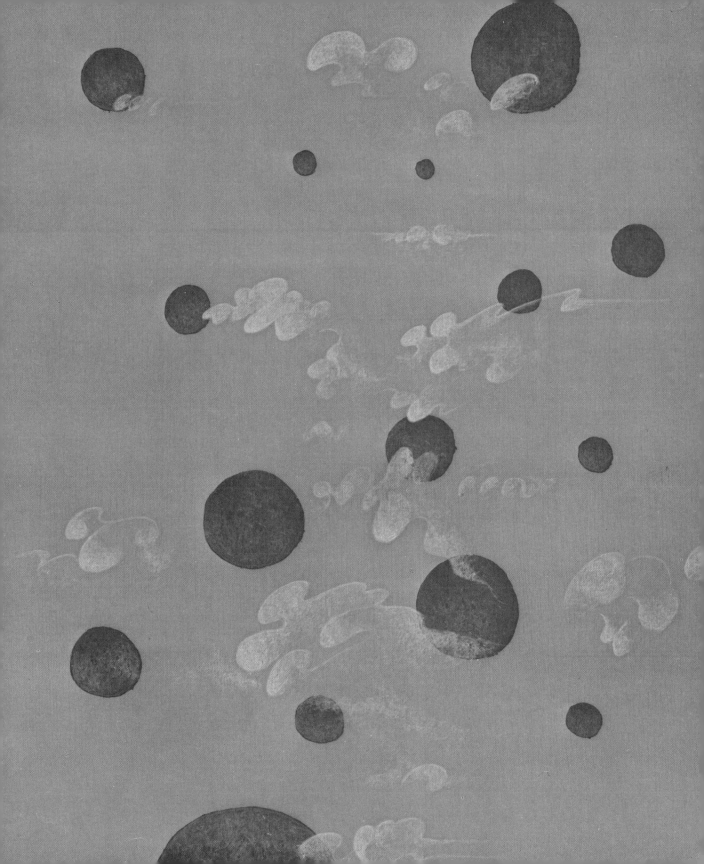

That was the first of many lessons Zeke and I had with Mr. Kendall.  We met almost every day, and it wasn't long before Zeke had mastered a whole list of words.  I decided to use *sit* and *stay* just like other people because I thought those were commands my parents might give him, and I wanted to be sure he would understand and obey.  But Zeke also learned to *pickle,* which meant *roll over,* and to *cucumber,* which meant *come.*  When I said, *"ragtime band,"* he knew that if he barked he'd get a biscuit.  Even Rex learned what *ragtime band* meant, and he'd get a biscuit, too.

Sometimes after our lessons Mr. Kendall would tell me about himself.  Mr. Kendall thought television was a waste of time ("never did like watching other people do things").  He didn't even own a radio.  And once when I mentioned a story I had read in the newspaper, he said that he'd lived through enough problems of his own ("sure don't need to read about everybody else's problems").

But he never talked about any problems.  Mostly he talked about his adventures.  He'd lived all over the country and had more different kinds of jobs than anyone I'd ever known.  He'd driven trucks ("the biggest babies you ever seen") and drilled for oil in Texas ("nearly struck it rich four times").  He'd been a hard-rock miner in Tennessee ("didn't last long at that one, no siree"), and he'd been a cowboy on a ranch in Colorado.

"A real cowboy?" I asked, trying to picture the old man who sat beside me riding herd and punching cattle just like the cowboys I saw in the movies.  "Did you fight rustlers and Indians, too?"

He laughed. "I'm not that old. That was before my time. But I did like being a cowboy. Never was happy spending my days indoors. I liked sleeping outside at night, under the stars—just me and the cattle and no people to get in the way."

"Don't you like people?"

"Sure. Some people. But there are others . . . You know how it is. They want to order you around all the time. Or they make you feel that nothing you do is ever good enough. Or they don't really care about you, just themselves. No, I like people who know how to let you be yourself and who like you when you are. Sometimes you don't meet many of those."

I knew what he meant. There were some people I wasn't myself with, not my usual comfortable self. They made me feel shy or nervous or clumsy or that, no matter what I did, it just wasn't right. Some people made me feel I had to show off. Then I didn't like myself very much. Some people made me feel just plain bad.

But there were other people who made me feel terrific. When I was with them, I wasn't afraid to be myself, to be happy or sad or silly or serious. And I felt the same way about them. "Why is that?" I wondered and, not knowing the answer, I added it to the list of questions I'd have to figure out some day.

Those few weeks before Christmas are some of the happiest I can remember and all because of Zeke. But he wasn't the only surprise that came my way. About a week before school vacation was to begin, I was in the kitchen pouring myself a glass of milk when my mother asked, "How would you like to go to Florida with Aunt Kit and Uncle Joe for the vacation?"

I almost spilled the milk. "Go to Florida for the vacation?" I repeated, simply amazed. "With Aunt Kit and Uncle Joe? And Phil, too?" Phil was my cousin and exactly my age. My mother smiled and nodded. "I'd love to!" I exclaimed. "Yes, yes, yes!"

I was so excited I couldn't help doing a little dance of joy around the kitchen.

"You know," my mother said, "your father and I won't be going?"

I stopped and looked at her. "Why not?"

"We can't take time off from work."

I thought for a moment. I'd never spent more than one night away from my parents. "Then maybe I shouldn't go either."

My mother smiled. "I think you should. You'll have a wonderful time." I knew she was right, and I was just about to hug her when I noticed Zeke napping under the kitchen table. "Oh," I said, suddenly re-membering, "I can't leave Zeke. I have to take care of him."

"Now you see why dogs are trouble," my mother said. "You can't just pick up and go when you want to. You have to think of them."

I reached down and patted Zeke's coat. "I don't mind," I said, "I love him. I really don't mind." But even so I couldn't help sighing, "Florida."

I could see my mother thinking about something. Then she said, "You don't have to worry about Zeke. Daddy and I will take care of him." Those were the very words I was hoping she would say, and I jumped up and kissed her.

"Oh, thank you, thank you," I sang, so excited I nearly knocked her off her chair. "Wait 'til I tell everyone I'm going to Florida!"

The night before I was to leave I had a hard time falling asleep. I got out of bed and sat down next to Zeke. He was curled up like a plate, but he unwound enough to put his chin in my lap. "Don't worry," I told him, "I'll be back before you know it. My mother and father will feed you and take you for walks. I guess they won't play with you and roll on the floor like I do, but two weeks isn't so long, is it? And maybe by the time I get home, they'll love you almost as much as I do." His only comment was a long, soft sigh.

The next morning we left for Florida. We took an airplane. When we stepped off the plane into sunshine and warmth, it seemed impossible that only hours before I had been in snow and cold. There were tall, thin palm trees everywhere. Phil and I decided that we would have to climb one and see if we could pick coconuts. On the way to our hotel I saw the ocean. It wasn't the ordinary ocean, it was the Florida ocean, just as the clear, blue sky wasn't the same old sky I

saw every day at home. Even the people on the street were more interesting because they were Florida people. Everything was new and special to me.

The first part of the vacation was terrific. Aunt Kit and Uncle Joe let Phil and me do pretty much what we wanted. We spent the days swimming in the ocean, jumping off the highest diving board at the hotel pool, and making friends with the other people who had come to vacation in the sun.

One day we all want to a Seminole Indian village. I saw a tortoise that was one hundred years old and a man who wrestled alligators and put them to sleep by rubbing their stomachs. Phil and I had our photographs taken with some parrots—red and green and yellow and purple ones—perched on our heads and arms. It was a wonderful day filled with people and things I had never seen before. I tried to remember every detail so I could tell everybody back home about it.

When New Year's Eve came, Phil and I stayed up until midnight with Aunt Kit and Uncle Joe and the other guests at the hotel. We had horns and noise-makers. At exactly twelve o'clock we all cheered and made all the noise we could. We were celebrating the coming of a brand new year. I thought that if it was as good as the end of the old year, there was no telling how many wonderful, extraordinary things might happen. Phil and I kissed each other, and I guess because we were both so happy we weren't even shy about it.

When we went up to our room that night, we were too excited to sleep. So we got into our pajamas and sat at the window watching the street below. There were crowds of people passing by and a traffic jam of honking cars and taxicabs. It looked like a party. We shouted down to some of the people. They heard us and shouted back, "Happy New Year!"

Even though I didn't know them and could hardly see their faces, I felt as if the whole world down there was my friend. So did Phil. We decided to stay up and watch the sun rise. But we must have fallen asleep because the next thing we knew Aunt Kit was saying, "It's morning," and waking us up.

She asked me if I wanted to call my parents and wish them Happy New Year. I placed the call myself and in a few moments heard my father's voice. "It's me! From Florida!" I shouted. "Happy New Year!" My mother got on the extension phone in their bedroom. I could picture them both exactly. In a breathless rush I told them everything I had seen and done. They laughed at how fast I was talking. I could hear how pleased they were that I was having a good time.

Then I asked about Zeke. For a minute, neither my mother nor father said anything. I knew something was wrong. "What is it?" I asked, my voice trembling. "Is he sick?"

"No," my father said. He didn't say anything else. "What is it then?" I asked again, really worried now. "He ran away."

I thought something was wrong with the telephone connection because my father couldn't possibly have

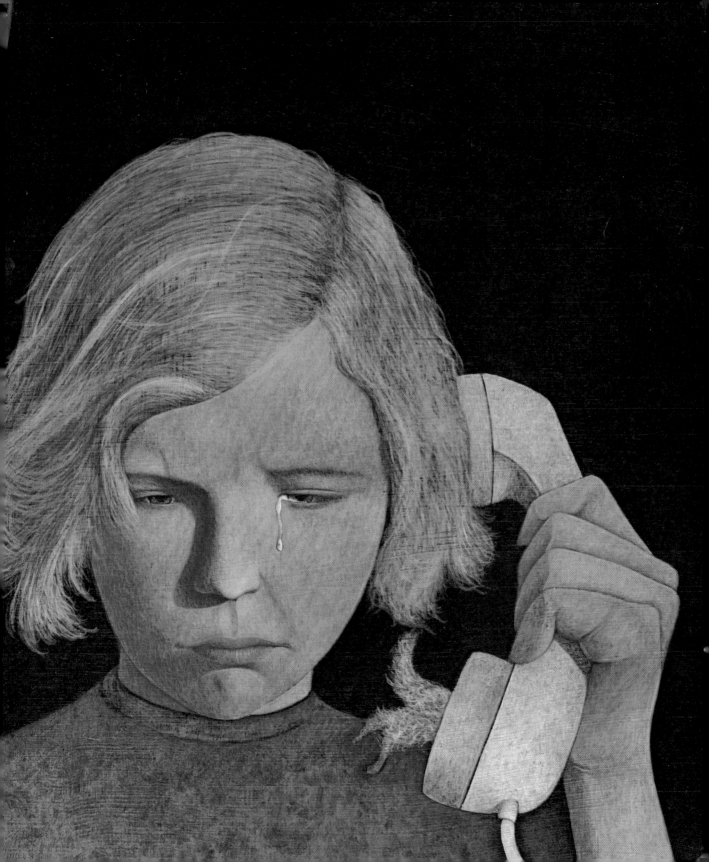

said what I heard. "I didn't hear you. What did you say?"

There was another long pause and then my mother said, "We put him out in the yard last week. When we went to let him in a few hours later, he was gone. Honey, we know how much he means to you. We've done everything possible. First, Daddy and I drove around the neighborhood for hours . . . calling and calling. We put up signs on all the lamp posts. We even put ads in the newspaper and had it announced on the radio. We offered a reward."

My father added, "We realized how upset you would be . . . . We've done everything we could."

By this time I wasn't even listening. I kept hearing the words, "He ran away," ringing in my ears.

Then I felt tears rolling down my cheeks, and I knew I was crying. "No!" I suddenly screamed, "No!" Unable to stop myself, I threw the telephone down on the bed and ran from the room. Aunt Kit called after me, but I didn't stop. I raced down the hotel corridor hardly able to see through my tears. Phil followed me and caught up with me as I opened a door that led to a stairway nobody ever used. "Go away," I told him, turning my face to the wall. "Just go away." He stood there, not knowing what to do, but he must have known that I needed to be alone because he finally left.

I sat down on the top stair and continued to cry. Something terrible had happened, and it was my fault. I had left him to go on a vacation. I loved him more than anything in the whole world, and now he was gone . . . and it was because of me. It would never have happened if I hadn't gone to Florida. I knew I should never have left him; he thought I was never coming back.

I couldn't believe it. Zeke wouldn't be at home waiting for me. He'd never again *orange* or lick my hand or look up at me with his one brown eye and his one blue eye.

The rest of my trip to Florida was ruined. Phil and I still jumped off the highest diving board and talked to new people and swam in the ocean, but it wasn't fun anymore. I called home twice. There was no sign of Zeke. He was never coming back. I kept thinking about walking into my house and not finding Zeke there. My dog Zeke. It wasn't true anymore.

When I got home, my parents were delighted to see me. They questioned me about everything that had happened. I was glad to tell them, but it wasn't half the fun it would have been if Zeke had been there. My mother said that one person had called about the ad in the paper. My parents rushed to her house to pick up Zeke—only it wasn't Zeke.

My mother and father said they would get me a new dog — any dog I wanted. But they didn't understand. I didn't want a new dog; I wanted Zeke.

That night I cried myself to sleep. The next morning I spent walking around calling Zeke. Maybe he would hear my voice and come running. I walked and called for two hours, but Zeke never came.

That afternoon I went to the park to find Mr. Kendall. He was the one person in the world who would understand how I felt. I felt very lonely and sad and angry. I still couldn't quite believe what had happened. And I still felt that it had been my fault.

When I arrived at the park, Mr. Kendall wasn't there yet. I sat down on the bench and waited. Then a woman walked over to me. I had seen her in the park on the days when I used to visit with Mr. Kendall.

"You're looking for the old man, aren't you?" she said. "He doesn't come here any more."

I looked at her in complete disbelief. It couldn't be happening. First Zeke, now Mr. Kendall. "What happened to him?" I asked.

"Nobody around here seems to know," she said.

Maybe he died. Or maybe he was hurt. I had never heard Mr. Kendall talk about friends or relatives; if he was hurt or sick, he might need help.

I ran home and called to my mother that I'd be back in a couple of hours. Then I started walking toward the woods where I knew Mr. Kendall lived. I had never seen his shack. It was hidden behind a huge grove of pine trees—even in the winter. I was frightened. Suppose he was dead. But I couldn't turn back. Mr. Kendall had been such a good friend when I needed him. Maybe he needed me now.

The road came to an end about a quarter of a mile before the shack. My heart was pounding as I stepped off the pavement and began to make my way along the path. The only sound I could hear was the sound of my own footsteps in the crunchy snow. I couldn't see what it was, but I heard an animal running through the brush. Then a cannonball of white fur rushed at me from the woods. It was Zeke! I couldn't believe it!

He was all over me, kissing me and jumping on me and licking me so that I couldn't tell where my tears of joy ended and his licks of happiness began. I was so happy I couldn't say anything. I just held him as tight as I could.

But I was confused. What was Zeke doing here? Why did Mr. Kendall have Zeke? If Zeke had run to his house, why hadn't Mr. Kendall called my parents or brought him back? A chill ran through my body as I thought unthinkable thoughts. Could Mr. Kendall have stolen Zeke? Could that have been why he stopped coming to the park . . . he didn't want to be seen? But that was impossible. Mr. Kendall was my friend and Zeke's too, and if he had taken Zeke, he must have had a very good reason.

I didn't have to wait very long to find out what had happened. I looked up and saw Mr. Kendall ahead of me on the path. He was walking on crutches.

"I had no way to let you know," he said. "The morning before Zeke arrived, I fell and broke my leg."

I was angry at myself. Of course there was a reason. But why hadn't he called? Then I remembered. Mr. Kendall didn't know where I lived; he didn't even know my last name. And all the ads . . . well, they had been on the radio and in the newspaper. Mr. Kendall didn't have a radio, and he didn't read the paper. The only thing he could have done was bring Zeke to the park. But with his bad leg, he couldn't get there.

"He must have thought you were never coming back," said Mr. Kendall. "You have a very smart dog there, you know. He must have run to the park thinking that you were there. When he didn't find you, he followed our scent here."

"He *is* smart," I said. "He's the smartest and most wonderful dog in the whole world." I hugged Zeke around the belly and buried my face in his fur. "Thank you, Mr. Kendall," I said, and kissed him on the cheek. Then I turned to Zeke. I didn't have a leash, but I said, *"Orange,* Zeke, *orange."* He jumped up and licked my face. *"Orange,* Zeke, *orange."* Zeke ran around me in a circle. Zeke wasn't going to *orange* and I didn't care. My dog Zeke and I were going home.